WELCOME TO BERMOODA

THE AMAZING
INCREDIBULL

written and illustrated by
MIKE LITWIN

ALBERT WHITMAN & COMPANY
CHICAGO, ILLINOIS

OTHER BOOKS IN THE WELCOME TO BERMOODA SERIES

Lost in Bermooda
Crown of the Cowibbean
The Big Cowhuna

Library of Congress Cataloging-in-Publication data is on file with the publisher.

Text and illustrations copyright © 2015 Mike Litwin
Hardcover edition published in 2015 by Albert Whitman & Company
Paperback edition published in 2016 by Albert Whitman & Company
ISBN 978-0-8075-8708-9

Printed in the United States of America
10 9 8 7 6 5 4 3 2 1 LB 20 19 18 17 16

For more information about Albert Whitman & Company,
visit our web site at www.albertwhitman.com.

for James

CONTENTS

1

AN INCREDIBULL GUESS

The world can be full of heroes, even in a peaceful paradise like Bermooda. Sometimes a hero is just a simple creature with a good heart. Sometimes a hero is just someone who shows up in the right place at the right time. And sometimes the hero has no idea who they are or what they are doing.

Chuck and Dakota Porter wouldn't really call themselves heroes. Chuck was just a little calf with a big thirst for excitement. Dakota was just a hu'man boy who wanted a quiet life with his adopted new family. Together, they always seemed to find adventure on this tiny tropical island, no matter how calm things appeared to be on the surface. Today, however, Chuck and Dakota were sitting in one place on Bermooda that was *not* calm: Leatherneck's Grill.

Leatherneck was a big hulk of a bull with a jolly voice, a gold ring in his nose, and a bold red shirt that was big enough to use as a blanket. His outdoor café sat at the edge of Bermooda Village, and it was always a popular place for calves to feast on grilled pineapple or slurp down fresh mango juice. But today his place was even busier than usual, with excited calves swarming around his bamboo counter like hungry ants on a drop of tropical cane sugar. Today, at exactly noon, Leatherneck would announce the winner of his IncrediBull Guessing Contest.

Leatherneck had started the contest to sell his new drink, the Avocadoberry Smoothie Punch. At the beginning of the month, he had filled a big jar with avocado seeds and placed it on the counter. Any time someone bought one of his new smoothies, they were allowed to guess how many seeds were in the jar by writing down their number on a big yellow ticket and putting it in a box. At the end of the month, whoever had the closest guess would win the chance to meet Norman Redmane—the creator of every calf's favorite superhero, IncrediBull.

Chuck and Dakota Porter sat at the table

closest to the guessing jar. Chuck was a huge fan of IncrediBull, and a chance to meet the artist would be like a dream come true. He had tried all kinds of ideas to find the closest guess. He had used math equations. He had weighed the jar. He had even surveyed other cows to see how many seeds *they* thought were in there. Today he was busily crumbling up leaves into little balls the same size as avocado seeds and dropping them into a wicker basket about the same size as the guessing jar. His tail twitched as he counted each ball, convinced this was one of his best ideas ever.

"Do you know how many smoothie punches you've bought this month?" Dakota asked as he sipped on Chuck's drink. Chuck wanted to put as many tickets as he could in the box, so he had bought Avocadoberry Smoothie Punches all month long.

"Nope," Chuck said without taking his eyes off his work. "I lost count."

"Over *six dozen*!" Dakota said, answering his own question.

Chuck paid little attention to Dakota. Noon was coming fast, and he wasn't finished counting all his fake avocado seeds yet.

"Is it really worth all this effort?" Dakota asked between slurps.

Chuck's tail stopped twitching. He froze mid-count and looked up. "*Of course* it's worth it!" he said. "Norman Redmane isn't just any artist. He's the creator of IncrediBull!" He pointed to the picture behind Leatherneck's guessing jar. It was a drawing of a red bull in a bright yellow superhero costume. He

5

wore a masked hood with a long cape, and his chest sported a logo in the shape of a cow head with a lightning bolt in it. The fiery supercow was swinging a fisted hoof into the air, and from his mouth came a word bubble that read: "Leatherneck's Smooooothies give me a PUNCH!"

"Yeah, I know." Dakota sighed. "I just don't see the big deal with IncrediBull. I mean, look at that ridiculous costume! It doesn't exactly look like something you'd find on Bermooda."

"Neither do you," Chuck reminded Dakota. "And his costume isn't any more ridiculous than yours."

Dakota couldn't help but agree. After all, he was the only hu'man to have ever been on Bermooda. The walking, talking animals that lived on the island all seemed to agree that hu'mans were legendary monsters that had died out years ago. When Chuck first found Dakota washed up on a sandbar, he'd disguised Dakota in cowmouflage—a cow costume stitched together from blankets, sponges, and coconut shells. To keep panic from gripping the island, Dakota had continued to wear the ugly disguise ever since.

"All right, little partners!" Leatherneck's cheerful voice boomed. "Thirty seconds until noon! Twenty-nine! Twenty-eight!"

"Wait!" Chuck cried, quickly turning back to his basket. "I'm not finished yet!" But in his hurry to finish counting, he accidentally knocked over the basket and scattered leaves everywhere.

"Oh noooooo!" Chuck mooed. He got

down on all fours and grabbed frantically at the wadded leaves, which were already starting to swirl away in the swift midday breeze. "Quick! Stall him! Get him to stop the countdown!"

"What do you want me to do?" Dakota asked. "Stop time?"

"Twenty-three...twenty-two...twenty-one..." Leatherneck counted down.

"Fifty-five! Fifty-six! Fifty-seven!" Chuck called out, trying to keep count of the escaping leaves. "Fifty-seven! Wait, did I already say fifty-seven? Grab that one! Fifty-seven! I mean—fifty-eight...plus those five is sixty-four...No, wait—sixty-three! What happened to the other four that were right here?"

Leatherneck reached his final countdown. "Ten...nine...eight..."

"Gahhh! Ninety-two! Eighty-seven! Eleventy-three!" Chuck blurted out random numbers in a panic.

"Oh, for crying out loud!" Dakota snapped. "Give me that!" He plucked the yellow ticket out of Chuck's shirt pocket, wrote down a number, and dropped it in the box just as the countdown ended.

Calves crowded around the guessing jar. Chuck eagerly chewed on his own hoof as Leatherneck counted out the seeds in the jar and then slowly flipped through the yellow tickets in the box. There were a lot of guesses, and it felt like the judging took forever.

"And the winner is..." Leatherneck finally announced, "...*Dakota Porter*, with the exact guess of *seventy-four*! Seventy-four, right...on...

da...NOSE!" Leatherneck poked the squishy sponge nose covering Dakota's face.

Chuck stared at Dakota in disbelief as all the losing calves lumbered away, grumbling slightly. He stood with his mouth hanging open as the last of his precious leaves blew away from around his hooves.

"*Seventy-four?*" Chuck asked. "I spent *all month* trying to figure out the right number, and you win it just by *guessing*? What made you think of seventy-four?"

Dakota scratched his head and shrugged as he pawed the ground with his fake hoof. "That's the number of smoothies you bought this month," he said.

II

Chuck and Dakota sat down the next morning for one of Mama Porter's famous breakfasts of pineapples, crushed oats, and coconut yogurt before heading out for their visit with the famous artist. Dakota didn't care as much about the contest as Chuck did, of course. So he'd given his prize-winning ticket to his brother. After all, Chuck *was* IncrediBull's biggest fan. But even though the ticket was only for one, Chuck insisted that Dakota come along. Chuck was sure that Norman Redmane wouldn't mind an extra visitor. Their little sister Patty begged to come too, but Chuck was afraid that two extra guests might be pushing it.

"This is awesome!" Chuck squealed as they began their walk to Norman Redmane's studio. "Thanks for the ticket!"

Chuck carried his collection of cowmic books in a big stack, hoping that the artist would sign every one. As they trotted along, he kept pushing issues of *IncrediBull* under Dakota's nose.

"How can you not see the big deal with IncrediBull?" Chuck asked. "He's so cool! By day, he's Taurus Tate, mild-mannered millionaire. But by night, he protects the island from evildoers!" He shoved a copy of *IncrediBull #57* in front of Dakota. On the cover, the flashy red-and-yellow bull was shouting *"Geronimoooo!"* while bursting through a wall like a huge bolt of lightning. "Look! He can fly at the speed of lightning! He can zap evildoers right into the ground!"

"Take a look around." Dakota sighed, stretching out his arms. The gentle sound of waves echoed at them from every direction, and the salty breeze tickled their noses as it ruffled through the pink oleander flowers. "Waves. Sand. Bamboo. Flowers. This is paradise! There are no 'evildoers' here! It's like I said yesterday. This 'superhero' just doesn't look like something from a tropical island."

"Well, duuuuhh!" Chuck blurted out, rolling his eyes. "He's *not* from a tropical island. He's from another world! He jumped to Bermooda in a lightning bolt from *over the moon*! Golly, don't they have cowmic books where you're from?"

"Sure," Dakota shrugged his shoulders. "I just think they're kind of silly, that's all. The dramatic language...the goofy names... the fact that no one can see through their terrible disguises," he said, adjusting his cow mask.

"IncrediBull isn't silly," he said, "and Norman Redmane is legen-dairy!"

"Really?" Dakota asked. "What's he like?"

"Well...no one's really sure," Chuck admitted. "Leatherneck is the only one I know who's ever met him. He mostly keeps to himself and hardly ever leaves the house. He mails all his cowmic books to be printed. That's why this visit is such a big deal!"

Redmane's studio was kind of hidden. They could only find it by following a special map that came with the winning ticket. After about an hour of walking, the map led them up a small hill to a big house half buried in the side of Mount Maverick.

"Is this it?" Dakota grimaced.

It was not what they had expected. If Norman Redmane was legendary, one would never guess it from the outside of his studio. The sloping tile roof was falling apart. The rickety wooden fence in front looked like it might collapse if it were breathed on. The door was nearly hidden behind tall clumps of weedy beach grass, and the yard greeted them with a collection of warning signs that read: PRIVATE PROPERTY, KEEP OUT, GO AWAY and THIS MEANS YOU!

"This fella really does keep to himself, doesn't he?" Dakota said, reading all the signs. "Looks like Leatherneck might be his only friend. Maybe we should just 'keep out' and 'go away.'"

"He has lots of fans," Chuck said, trudging through the overgrown yard. "He probably just likes his privacy. Besides, we *won* the chance to visit."

Chuck balanced his stack of cowmic books in one arm as he knocked on the door. "He'll be happy we're here. You'll see."

Chuck's knocking was answered by the opening of a little window in the front door. A pair of dark eyes surrounded by red fur appeared on the other side, along with a sharp voice that barked, "Who are you? What's the password?"

Password? Chuck thought. *The ticket didn't say anything about a password!*

"Ummm...my name is Chuck Porter," he said. "We won a guessing contest at Leatherneck's Café?"

The face on the other side of the door squinted at them suspiciously. "The deal was for just *one* of you," he said.

"This is my brother, Dakota," Chuck stammered. "He really wanted to come along. He's...ummm...a big IncrediBull fan too." He nudged Dakota with his hoof.

"Oh. Yeah," Dakota sputtered. "'*Geronimoooo!*'"

The dark eyes shifted back and forth, as if searching for even more visitors. "All right," he finally said, sighing.

The door opened, and they were greeted by a round, tubby bull slurping down a bowl of coconut pudding. He was as big as Leatherneck, with wide, chubby legs that held up an even wider, chubbier body. He was covered from head to tail with shaggy fur that was the same fiery-red color as IncrediBull himself. A scraggly mane of curls blossomed from atop his head and around his neck, and his burly red belly was barely covered by a tightly stretched green tee shirt and a dirty yellow button-up that was too small to button.

This is Norman Redmane? Dakota thought. *What a slob!*

"Come on in," the big red bull said. His voice wasn't deep and jolly like Leatherneck's. This bull's voice was high and raspy, and sounded like he had a lump of gravel in his throat. He spoke very quickly, and he said the word "dude"...a *lot*.

"Hurry up, little dudes...and don't touch anything."

Chuck and Dakota hurried through the door and found that the inside didn't look much nicer than the outside. A sea of dust floated in the air, glowing in the sunlight that peeked through the faded yellow curtains. The ceiling was cracked; the windows were grimy; and the withered plants decorating the house looked like they hadn't been watered in ages.

"*Lo'hai*, Mister Redmane. It's really an honor to meet you." Chuck tried his best to shake hooves without dropping his cowmic books. "Thanks for the tour. *Moohalo*."

"No, dude...just call me Norman," he answered, dropping pudding on his shirt as he ate. "And sorry about the whole 'password' thing, little buds. Sometimes you just never know who's showing up at your door."

Dakota couldn't help but chuckle. From the looks of the place, no one had shown up at this door in a long time.

Norman finished his pudding with a burp. He tossed the empty bowl onto the couch, where it landed with a dusty *poof.* "All right, little dudes," he said, clapping his hooves together. "Ready for the tour? You can look at anything you want, but like I said...don't touch anything. Cool?"

Norman began the tour of his huge, unkempt house. The place was filled with strange items that Chuck recognized from the pages of *IncrediBull.* A bony sword from one issue, a magic crystal from another... They were displayed all over the house, like artifacts in a very messy museum.

"Wow! Is that the Mask of Power from issue #157?" Chuck babbled, gazing at a wooden mask hanging in the hallway.

"Yup." Norman nodded. "And check this

out!" He removed a flowered necklace from a wooden tiki statue near the kitchen door. "It's the Eternity Lei from issue #34! Don't wear it though...it might send you light years into the future!"

Chuck was so thrilled that he began spilling copies of *IncrediBull* from his stack of cowmic books all over the stained rug on the floor.

"Whoa...Easy, dude," Norman said. "You're making a mess."

Each jumbled room had more and more keepsakes from IncrediBull's many adventures. Chuck had read every issue of *IncrediBull*, so each time Norman showed him something from one of the stories, Chuck happily nodded his head.

Dakota, on the other hand, had never

read a single issue of *IncrediBull* and didn't understand the excitement over a bunch of junk. "So...you find all this stuff and then you write IncrediBull stories about it?" he asked.

"Maybe." Norman turned slowly and raised his left brow. "Or *maybe* the stories *really happened*. What do you think?" He winked playfully, but Dakota wasn't sure if he was kidding.

Dakota found something else on the tour much more impressive. As it turned out, Norman wasn't just a fantastic artist. He was also quite the inventor. Each cluttered room was filled with odd little machines he had built himself—crazy contraptions made of levers and gears and pulleys that performed the simplest tasks.

The kitchen had an automatic pancake

flipper. The study room had a gizmo that turned book pages. The den had a device that turned on all the sunglobes at once from a long mahogany handle near the door. As they navigated around the stacks of odds and ends piled along the tour route, Dakota wondered why a creative cow like Norman hadn't invented a machine that could clean the house.

"And now comes the best part," Norman said, leading them to a set of spiral stairs in the living room. "This is the part you came to see." Chuck and Dakota followed Norman as he climbed the creaky bamboo stairs to an overhead landing with a single red door. "My friends, I present to you...the *Drawing Room*."

Norman swung open the door to reveal what was easily the most cluttered room in the house. This was obviously where he spent most of his time. The place was filled with dirty dishes from countless meals that were eaten while drawing. Old issues of *IncrediBull* were stacked everywhere. On one side of the room was a wide drawing table surrounded by overstuffed shelves crammed full of papers, books, posters, and potted plants that looked even more lifeless than the ones downstairs.

Aside from a small window, the only real light in the room came from a sunglobe whose bulb dimly flickered above the drawing table. There were no souvenirs of IncrediBull's adventures here, except for an ugly stone statue perched on the top shelf near the door.

"Hey! Isn't that the Freaky Tiki?" Chuck

said, setting down his stack of cowmic books. "The haunted statue from issue #66?"

"Yeah, dude!" Norman said. "But I can't take that one down to show you. It's pretty heavy. Besides, you know...it's *haunted*."

Chuck and Dakota snickered as they inched closer to the drawing table, being careful not to touch anything. The table was covered with artwork for the upcoming issue of *IncrediBull*.

Wow, Chuck thought, *this is where it all happens.* He could just imagine how many hours Norman spent hunched over this table, bringing IncrediBull's adventures to life. His eager ears listened as Norman described the newest story being told in the pictures spread across the drawing table.

Norman was bizarre for an adult. He

seemed more like an overgrown calf stuck in a bull's body as he excitedly went on about heroes, villains, and epic tales that he had yet to finish putting on paper. And despite the fact that he wouldn't let them touch anything, Norman Redmane had turned out to be a pretty nice fellow. It made Dakota wonder why all those angry warning signs were posted in his yard. Maybe he just needed to get out more often.

Dakota strolled over to the window and looked down at the steep roof of the house that curved out below. "Have you ever thought about going to the beach once in a while?" he asked. "It's really very pretty." He blew on the dusty windowsill and a little cloud curled up into the air, tickling his nose. Dakota let out a thunderous sneeze that almost rocketed the cow mask right off his face.

"There's lots of fresh air too," he added with a sniffle.

"Putting IncrediBull's adventures on paper is kind of a full-time thing, little dude." Norman shrugged, pointing to a poster of IncrediBull on the wall. "IncrediBull is my whole life."

Among the scattered artwork, Chuck spied a drawing of an odd little character he'd never seen before. It had a bowl-shaped head, skinny mechanical arms, and a single wheel where its legs would have been. Without thinking, he plucked the page from the table. "What's this?" he asked. "A new villain?"

"*Don't touch*," Norman said, snatching the

page from Chuck's hoof. "It's not a villain. It's an *autocow*. I built it to clean the house, wash dishes, run errands...all the work that a real cow would do."

A robot! Dakota thought to himself. *So Norman* did *invent something to clean the house!*

"Anyway, one day I sent it down to the village to deliver some cowmic books, and it never came back." Norman's eyes glazed over, like a sad calf who had lost his favorite toy. "Someone stole my best invention ever. A machine that does all your chores, but never gets tired because it runs on boltage... just like the sunglobes."

Norman pointed to the glass lightbulb over his head, still flickering as it dangled from the ceiling. Dakota scratched his head and suddenly recalled that *every* sunglobe in the house had been flickering like that—blinking and sputtering with an unsteady glow in each room on the tour.

"Are you sure someone stole it? Maybe it just ran out of power," Dakota suggested. "Your sunglobes are flickering in every room. Are you having problems with your boltage?"

"No, dude," Norman said, shaking his head. *"That's from the aliens."*

RESPONSIBULL

"Aliens?" Dakota echoed. He suddenly felt very uncomfortable.

"Yeah, dude," Norman jabbered on. "From *IncrediBull* issue #143! When Zimrod and his alien race flew over Bermooda."

Dakota had no idea what issue #143 was all about, but Chuck nodded in agreement. Norman looked upward as if he could see right through the ceiling. "They're still out there somewhere," he said, "and they're up to something."

"Is that...also the reason why all your plants are dead?" Dakota asked.

"No, that's from all the waves coming out of the radio tower," Norman scoffed. "Remember *IncrediBull* issue #81? The one called 'Radio Silence'? That's right...The ocean isn't the only thing making waves, my friend."

Norman turned his head toward the window. "There's all kinds of craziness out there," he said. "That's why Bermooda needs a hero like IncrediBull."

There's all kinds of craziness in here too, Dakota thought to himself.

"You guys know about the *hu'man*, right?" Norman suddenly asked, pointing both hooves at them.

"The hu'man?" Chuck and Dakota repeated. Dakota's face felt hot and flushed. Chuck's back stiffened. Did Norman know about *their* secret too?

"At last year's Boomflower Festival," Norman continued. "Remember? There was that big storm and some crazy hu'man monster was up on the rocks!"

Chuck and Dakota remembered it all too well. It had happened right after Dakota arrived on Bermooda. But the whole thing was just part of a plan by wealthy Wilhelm Wellington to take control of the island.

"But that wasn't a real hu'man," Dakota said, breathing a sigh of relief. "It was just someone in a costume playing a prank. They said so in the moospaper."

"You actually believe the moospaper?"

Norman laughed. "They never get the facts right! I have proof...some feathers and a spiky bone! Hold on, I'll go get them!"

Norman hurried off to find his proof. Dakota turned to Chuck and quietly asked, "Norman knows IncrediBull isn't *real*, right?"

Chuck gazed up at the flickering sunglobe, and Dakota knew exactly what he was thinking. Chuck liked believing in fantastic things, so it was no surprise when he replied, "Do you really think all the flickering could be from—?"

"Aliens?" Dakota interrupted. "Are you kidding? The bulbs are probably just loose. I'll bet Norman forgot to tighten them." He waved his arms at the surrounding clutter. "I mean, look at this place! What a mess! You know, a little responsibility would go a long way."

Grinning, Dakota jumped up onto Norman's chair. He jokingly put his hands on his hips and puffed up his chest, posing like a superhero.

"Zounds!" he bellowed in a deep, funny voice. "It appears that some dirty devil has littered this room! The sloppy scoundrel has starved these plants of water and failed to tighten the sunglobe!" He thrust his right hand high above his head. "*This* looks like a job for...ResponsiBull!"

Chuck's eyes narrowed. "Stop it," he muttered in a flat voice, afraid that Norman might hear him poking fun.

"Watch, my young friend!" Dakota pointed at Chuck. "Watch ResponsiBull save the day with his powers of basic upkeep!"

Dakota began scaling the shelves like a

ladder. They squeaked
as he slowly climbed
to the top and
reached for the bulb
on the ceiling.

"Get down!" Chuck
said. "Norman said not
to touch anything!"

"Almost...got it..."
Dakota said, stretching his
arm out toward the sun-
globe. The shelves began to
creak and moan. Dakota
was not terribly heavy,
but Norman's shelves
were crammed so full
that they couldn't
handle any more

weight. The creak turned into a *CRACK!* as the overloaded shelves splintered and broke. Dakota tumbled to the floor with a heap of broken shelves and clutter trailing behind him.

"What was that noise?" Norman called out as he bounded back into the room. He stopped inside the doorway, gawking through a dusty haze at Dakota and the mound of rubble. "Dude! What happened here? See, *this* is why I have all those signs outside!"

Norman was so upset that he didn't even notice the Freaky Tiki statue still teetering on what was left of the shelf above him. The heavy statue wobbled for a moment, then dropped onto Norman's head with a loud *CLUNK!*

Chuck and Dakota both winced. That

clunk even *sounded* painful. Norman weaved back and forth on his hooves for a moment. A strange smile crossed his face as his eyes rolled back in his head and he collapsed face-first into the mess on the floor.

"Now you've done it, you *kau'pai*!" Chuck yelled. "You knocked him out! You knocked out a famous artist!"

Chuck waved a hoof in front of Norman's face.

"Norman?" Chuck asked. "Norman, can you hear us?"

"Norman?" the shaggy red bull repeated. He stared blankly at Chuck. "Who's Norman? My name is Taurus. Taurus Tate."

"Taurus Tate?" Dakota said to Chuck. "Isn't that IncrediBull's secret identity?"

"*Great grazing!*" Norman shouted. "They

40

know my secret identity!" He leaped to his feet, turned away from them, and began speaking into thin air. "But the question is, do they know of my powers as well? Or my home planet of Cowpernia?"

Dakota looked around the room. "Umm... who's he talking to?"

Norman spun on his hooves to face them. He studied Dakota for a moment. Then the look on his face softened, as if he had just recognized an old friend.

"Fantasti-Calf!" Norman smiled at Dakota. "I almost didn't recognize you without your costume! Of course you knew it was me! But this doesn't look like Tate Tower! Where are we?" Before either of them could answer, he rushed off downstairs.

"What's he talking about?" Dakota

whispered to Chuck. "Who's Fantasti-Calf? What's Tate Tower?"

Chuck tossed a copy of *IncrediBull #35* at Dakota. The cover showed a picture of a small brown calf in a blue costume, lifting a huge boulder over his head. "Fantasti-Calf is IncrediBull's sidekick," Chuck said. "Tate Tower is the mansion where IncrediBull lives." They listened as Norman darted from room to room downstairs. "Don't you get it? *He thinks he* is *IncrediBull!*"

"Okay, no problem." Dakota held up his hands. "We'll just explain everything."

Norman returned to the Drawing Room and put his hooves on his hips. "What kind of villainy has happened here, my young friend?" he said, eyeing the wreckage on the floor.

"Well, you see," Dakota began, "I was

climbing those shelves there. To fix the sunglobe, you know? And then the shelves started to creak, and—"

"Ah yes!" Norman bellowed, cutting him off. "The sunglobes! I've seen them flickering in every room! I suspect the evil work of Zimrod and his alien race!"

"No, no...there are no aliens," Dakota said, "and I'm not Fantasti-Calf! I'm just—"

But Norman wasn't listening. "Come, Fantasti-Calf!" he called out, darting to the window.

"Where are you going?" Chuck asked.

"There's no telling what kind of scheme Zimrod is up to!" Norman answered. "He could be harvesting boltage for his entire alien fleet! This could be the end of Bermooda as we know it! It's time to fly into action!"

"Wait!" Dakota said as Norman squeezed through the window. "You're not IncrediBull! You can't..."

It was too late. Before anyone could tell Norman that he couldn't fly, he leaped from the windowsill with a hearty, "*Geronimoooooo!*"

Chuck and Dakota scurried to the window in time to see Norman tumble down the curved roof underneath. He bumped and bounced all the way down, knocking off tiles in every direction before finally sailing off the bottom corner of the roof and plummeting into the weeds with an "Oof!" No sooner had he landed than the whole corner of the rickety roof fell off, landing on him with a big, dusty thud.

Chuck and Dakota scrambled down the stairs and out the front door. There Norman was, pinned under a pile of rubble.

"Blast!" Norman coughed as he pushed on the roof. "It's too heavy! Fantasti-Calf! Quick! Use your superstrength!"

"I don't have superstrength!" Dakota blurted out.

Chuck's tail twitched furiously as he tried to think. "Ooh! I have an idea!" he said, racing into the house.

Dakota tried his best to lift the wreckage off Norman while waiting for Chuck. He pushed and pulled on the big chunk of roof until his face muscles strained and sweat poured out of him. But it was no use. The rubble wasn't moving.

Chuck finally returned, dragging the

long handle from the gadget that turned on all the sunglobes in Norman's den.

"Put this end under the roof," Chuck said, laying the mahogany lever over a big rock in the yard. "Then we'll hang on the other end until our weight lifts the roof up."

Dakota put one end of the pole under the debris. Then they both jumped up and grabbed the other end. They hung with their feet swinging in the air, but nothing moved.

"Come on, Fantasti-Calf," Chuck joked. "Put some *calf muscle* into it!"

"We're too light!" Dakota said. "We need something heavier!"

"Heavier?" Chuck repeated, his tail twitching again. "Okay! Just hang out here." He dropped to the ground and disappeared back into the house. After a few minutes,

Dakota heard a loud *thumpity-thumpity, thump, thump, thump* from inside, followed by Chuck rolling the heavy stone tiki statue out the door and into the yard.

"The Freaky Tiki!" Norman yelped. "Have you gone mad? That thing is cursed!"

Chuck and Dakota ignored Norman's protests. They tied the heavy statue to the lever and then hung on the end again. The extra weight was enough to lift the roof, and Norman slowly crawled out.

"I can't fly at super-speed," Norman panted as he dusted himself off. "And you don't have superstrength. There can only be one explanation for this."

Thank goodness, Dakota thought. *Maybe that tumble down the roof knocked some sense into him.*

Norman thundered, "Some fiend has stolen my powers of flight and speed, and robbed you of your superstrength as well!"

Dakota sighed, shook his head, and buried his face in his hands.

Norman put a firm hoof on Dakota's shoulder. "You'd better head home and lie low, my young friend," he said, glaring off into the distance. "The flickering lights will have to wait. It appears we have greater problems. Someone...is *stealing powers*."

"Oh brother," Dakota groaned.

4

THE LESSON

The next day, Chuck and Dakota tried to return to life as normal. After all, that was what "IncrediBull" had told them to do. But when they went to school, nearly every calf wanted to know about Norman Redmane. They bombarded Chuck and Dakota with questions:

"What does he look like?"

"Is he nice?"

"Did he sign your books?"

The Porter calves only answered with long faces. Dakota didn't want to think about the accident he'd caused, and Chuck didn't need any reminder that he had completely forgotten his big stack of *IncrediBull* cowmic books in Norman's studio. They did their best to ignore the questions and focus on Miss Ginger's science lesson.

Miss Ginger was a young, white heifer with a cheery smile, a pleasant voice, and a collection of sundresses that were almost as bright as the sun itself. Today she was trying to teach the calves about boltage—how it was generated by the wind-powered spinners in Wellington Field, carried all over the island through big underground wires, and eventually used to power sunglobes like the one in the schoolhouse ceiling. But when she turned the switch, the glass bulb only flickered and gave off a weak glow, just like the ones in Norman's house.

"That's strange," Miss Ginger said. "I wonder why it's doing that."

"The boltage was like that at our house too," said Chuck's sister, Patty, from the row of younger calves at the front of the class. "The lights flickered all night."

The rest of the calves in class joined her in agreement:

"So did ours!"

"Mine too!"

"Same here!"

Dakota reached out his foot and nudged Chuck at the desk in front of him. "Maybe it's *aliens*," he mumbled.

"Someone should tell Wilhelm Wellington," griped a fuzzy yellow calf in the back of the class. "After all, he owns the windspinners, along with just about everything else."

"That may be true, Muster," Miss Ginger said, switching off the sunglobe. "Which brings me to another important lesson for today. Wilhelm Wellington *does* own much here on Bermooda, but there's one thing he *doesn't* own. Can anyone tell me what that is?"

"The moon?" guessed Patty. The whole room laughed lightly, but no one could answer Miss Ginger's question.

"*You*." Miss Ginger smiled, pointing her hoof at the class. "He may own lots of things, but he can never own *you*."

It occurred to Dakota how no one on Bermooda had any pets. No fish in bowls, no birds in cages, no pigs in pens. Every being on the island was a free creature, and none of them could ever be *owned* by another. He rested his chin in his hand and gazed out the window thinking about this. Suddenly, he spotted a bright red-and-yellow figure dashing out from the palmetto bushes and hiding behind a grove of palm trees in the distance.

Dakota nudged Chuck again. "Did you see that?" he whispered.

"And no matter how much Wilhelm Wellington may possess," Miss Ginger continued, "this little island will always need the skills of talented, hard-working calves like you."

Miss Ginger was right. Even a tropical paradise like Bermooda needed lots of folks doing their parts to keep everything running. It needed farmers like Cotton Cattleman, the hearty bull who tended to the fields. It needed sea captains like Skipper Morton, the salty old fish who harvested sea grass. It needed mechanics like Soward Seawell, the brilliant flying pig who fixed machines and dusted crops with his airplane.

"Each resident of Bermooda is gifted with a talent...a skill they can offer to help our society," Miss Ginger said. Her bright sundress swished as she strolled up and down the aisles of desks. "As you grow, you will each learn what your special talent is. That makes you all *individuals*—special, important, and more valuable than anything owned by Wilhelm Wellington."

Chuck and Dakota listened intently as

Miss Ginger encouraged the calves. But their attention was suddenly broken by a sharp whisper from outside: "Psst! *PSST!* Fantasti-Calf!"

Dakota's heart sank. He and Chuck both slowly leaned their heads out the bamboo window frame and looked underneath. There, doing his best to hide in a bed of red hibiscus flowers, was Norman Redmane wearing the silliest getup they'd ever seen.

It looked like Norman had fashioned an IncrediBull costume with whatever he could find around his house. He had ditched the green shirt and was now squeezed into a striped yellow swimsuit. Pinned to the front of the suit was an IncrediBull logo torn from the poster on Norman's wall. A long yellow cape with little palm trees on it—which Dakota recognized as one of the faded curtains from Norman's front windows—was tied around his neck and stretched up over his face like a hood. The final flare to his outfit was a curved yellow mask that looked like a crescent moon pointing up toward the sky. Chuck and Dakota gawked in disbelief.

"What are you *doing* here?" Dakota spat out in a whisper.

"I went to the place where Tate Tower is supposed to be," Norman said. "There's nothing there but an old lighthouse! I've had to return to that horrible, messy house where we first lost our powers. It may not be Tate Tower, but that's no matter. There's work to be done."

"What kind of work?" Chuck asked softly.

"Finding out who stole our powers, of course," Norman scoffed. "Along with any other heroic deeds that are needed. Come, Fantasti-Calf!"

"I can't come with you!" Dakota hissed. "*I'm in school*!"

"Mister Porter!" a voice rang from the other side of the room. "*Both* Mister Porters! Is there something more interesting outside the window than inside this class?"

57

Chuck and Dakota whipped their heads around to see Miss Ginger glaring through her long eyelashes. "No, ma'am," they answered together. They didn't dare tell her about the fake superhero outside. Miss Ginger went back to her lesson.

"All right, my young friend," Norman finally uttered in a hushed voice. "Return to your studies! And worry not! I'll find the villain! Geronimooooo!"

Chuck and Dakota watched as Norman bounded back to the palm trees, jerked his head around, and then dove into the bushes from which he had first appeared. His round belly made a soft *crash* in the leaves. They heard him cry out *"Ouch!"* as palmetto thorns pricked him all over.

"Okay, see?" Dakota nodded at Norman's

cape as it slithered into the greenery. "Now *that* looks like a superhero from a tropical island."

5

DANGER NEVER STOPS

"We can't just ignore this," Chuck said after class. "We have to do something before Norman gets into trouble."

"So what if Norman thinks he's IncrediBull?" Dakota shrugged. "That's not my problem."

"Oh, yes it is!" Chuck growled, grabbing Dakota's shirt. "*You* were the one who just had to climb Norman's shelves, and *you* were the one who dropped a statue on his head!"

No matter how much Dakota wanted to deny it, Chuck was right. This had all happened because of him. Keeping Norman safe until they could bring his memory back was *his* job now. It was the kind of thing ResponsiBull would do.

Finding Norman was not terribly difficult. A chunky red bull running around in a mask and cape was the kind of thing that stood out on Bermooda. They tracked him to Bovine Bluff, a small cliff on the east side of the mountain. He was crouched in a yellow hydrangea bush with a hollow, cone-shaped device plunked into his ear.

Norman spotted them coming and waved them over. When they came closer, they noticed a canvas tool belt filled with strange gadgets wrapped around his waist.

"What's with the belt?" Dakota asked. He had listened to Chuck prattle on about IncrediBull and his awesome powers, but he didn't remember anything about a tool belt stuffed with thingamabobs.

"It's my mootility belt." Norman beam-ed, pulling the cone from his ear with a little pop. "These inventions will aid us in our fight against villainy!"

He showed off the first two gadgets on the belt. "This Grapplehoof allows us to climb steep walls and grab objects from afar," he said, pointing at a claw attached to a bamboo handle with a long cord. Then he held up a V-shaped horn with fabric wrapped around it. "The Mooberang here

can be thrown at great distance and will always return to you."

He then held up the cone that had been stuck in his ear. "And *this*! The Bullhorn!" he said. "This ear funnel gives us the hearing of a tropical bat!"

"So...it's the IncrediBelt!" Dakota joked. In truth, he thought the gadgets were pretty clever.

Chuck was far less impressed. "But

IncrediBull doesn't *have* a mootility belt!" he whined in a shrill voice.

"When IncrediBull's powers are *stolen*, he has to make certain *adjustments*," Norman snapped. "Danger never stops...and neither can I."

Chuck was aware that Norman wasn't really IncrediBull, but he still hated the idea of his superhero having anything different from how it was in the cowmic books. However, the mootility belt gave Dakota a sense of hope. All those inventions meant that Norman's memory must still be in there somewhere.

"Actually, that's what we wanted to talk to you about," Dakota started. "There *is no* danger here on Bermooda. And you're *not* IncrediBull. Your name is—"

"Shhh! Not so loud!" Norman covered the bullhorn with a hoof and whispered harshly. "You never know who might be listening! No one can know that Taurus Tate is my secret identity! Speaking of which..."

Norman dug into a pouch on the back of his mootility belt and pulled out a long scrap of blue fabric with two holes cut in it. "Take this," he said, stuffing it into Dakota's hand.

Dakota wrinkled his nose. "What's this?"

"Your mask, of course!" Norman said. "You can't wage war against evil without disguising your secret identity!"

Norman plunked the Bullhorn back into his ear and continued listening for danger.

"What am I supposed to do with *this*?" he whispered to Chuck, dangling the mask in front of him. "*Fight crime?* I'm no more a superhero than Norman is!"

"You don't have to *be* a superhero," Chuck said, taking the mask and tying it around Dakota's eyes. "You just have to *pretend*. How hard can that be?"

"Sorry, I'm already a little busy pretending to be a *cow*!" Dakota hissed.

Just then, a voice cried out so loudly that they didn't even need a bullhorn to hear it.

"Get me outta this thing!"

The three of them hurried to the edge of the bluff. Looking below for the voice's owner, they saw a familiar pig wrapped in a hammock stretched high up between two palm trees.

"Is that Soward Seawell?" Chuck asked.

Soward loved heights. The flying pig

always hung his rope hammock so far off the ground that he had to climb a tree just to get into it. Somehow though, he had become horribly tangled this time. Suspended in midair between the trees, Soward now looked very much like a big fly caught in a web of ropes.

"Durn blasted thing!" Soward snorted. *"You'll be the death of me!"*

With a heroic flair, Norman put one hoof on his hip and pointed at the wriggling pig with the other. "Look! A citizen in peril... trapped in a giant web!"

"It's a hammock," Dakota said.

"*Hammock*?" Norman echoed. "The name of some horrible spider queen, no doubt. We must free that struggling swine before Hammock returns!"

Norman sprang into action, tossing the Grapplehoof's claw into one of the trees holding Soward's hammock. "I'll use the Grapplehoof to swing down and pluck that pig from peril," he said, tightening the line.

"We could just climb down this side—" Dakota began. But it was too late. Norman gripped the bamboo handle and dove from the bluff like a monkey on a vine.

"Geronimooooooo!"

Norman's plan almost worked. First he swung right toward Soward, then he swung right past Soward. Then he swung right into the top of a banana tree twenty feet away.

Chuck and Dakota scurried down the easy slope of the bluff. When they reached the bottom, Soward was still dangling from his hammock. Norman was now also in a sticky situation, perched on the top of a banana tree. The top of the tree was bent toward the ground, tethered to a large root by Norman's Grapplehoof.

"Hold on!" Chuck said. "I'll get it!"

Before Norman could object, Chuck ran over to the Grapplehoof and kicked it loose from the root. Without the Grapplehoof holding things down, the banana tree sprang to life. It catapulted Norman through the air, flinging him back toward Soward like a big, red cannonball. Norman plowed right into Soward, ripping his hammock clean off the trees. Bull, pig, hammock, and bananas all rocketed through the air, crash-landing in a patch of prickly pear cactus.

Chuck and Dakota scrambled to the landing site and pulled both Soward and Norman out of the cactus.

"Some rescue!" Soward squealed. He pulled a big cactus thorn from his rump as Norman rose to his feet. "So much for a relaxing day in the old hammock! Look at it! It's all ripped to pieces—"

The flustered pig stopped short when he got a look at Norman's costume.

"My stars!" Soward gasped with his mouth hanging open. "It's IncrediBull! IncrediBull, in the flesh!" He tightly clutched his shredded hammock. Stuck between its frayed strands was a copy of *IncrediBull #88*.

Soward is an IncrediBull fan too? Dakota thought to himself. *How is he falling for this costume? Has everyone lost their minds?*

"My apologies, friend," Norman said, as he wound up his Grapplehoof. "I'm still learning the ropes, so to speak."

"Don't be ridiculous!" Soward bubbled. "It's not every day my curly tail gets saved by a real superhero." He started helping Norman pull prickly pear burs from his woolly red hide. "If ya ever need a favor—anything at all—ya just let me know. No questions asked."

"My pleasure, good citizen!" Norman said. "So long...until next issue!"

Soward hobbled off for home, so excited about meeting the "real-life" IncrediBull that he barely thought about the cactus thorns still stuck in his backside.

"As I said, Fantasti-Calf—*danger never stops*." Norman stuffed the Grapplehoof back in his belt. "Now follow me! There's wickedness to fight and lives to be saved! *Geronimooooooo!*"

With that, Norman bounded off into the thick tropical jungle. Chuck eagerly followed. Dakota slumped his shoulders.

This was going to be a rough day.

INCREDIBULL AND FANTASTI-CALF

The next day at school, every calf was talking about the burly red hero being spotted all over the island.

"Did you hear?" Patty Porter said. "IncrediBull pulled Bonnie Bovine's kite out of a tree!"

"I heard he stopped a fight between two surfcows," said her friend Lily.

"I heard he pulled Soward from a giant

spiderweb!" added a woolly little calf named Clayton.

"Don't be such a *kau'pai*!" Muster scoffed. "IncrediBull isn't even real! He's a cowmic book!"

"How do you explain all the IncrediBull sightings then?" Patty challenged him. "Whoever that bull is, no one's ever seen him before! He's the same color as IncrediBull! He has the same costume. How do *you* know it's not him?"

"Because there aren't any criminals on Bermooda!" Muster jeered. "So why would IncrediBull be here anyway?"

The bickering went on and on. Chuck and Dakota lounged in the grass near the short cobblestone wall of the playground, too exhausted to join in. They didn't need to hear the conversation to know about IncrediBull's activities. They had spent all afternoon and much of the night chasing after him.

No matter how peaceful Bermooda was, Norman seemed to have no trouble finding citizens in peril. A toucan choking on some fruit, a cow passed out from the afternoon heat, a monkey with its tail caught in the crook of a tree—they all needed "saving," and they were all amazed by the sudden appearance of IncrediBull and Fantasti-Calf.

Chuck and Dakota watched the puffy clouds roll over the playground and spoke very little—mostly because they were exhausted, but also because Chuck was feeling a bit jealous.

"Why do *you* get to be Fantasti-Calf?"

Chuck finally mumbled as he paged through his only remaining copy of *IncrediBull*. "You don't even *like* IncrediBull!"

"Do you think I'm *enjoying* this?" Dakota said. "If it were up to me, you'd be Fantasti-Calf."

"Norman doesn't even know I exist!" Chuck went on. "All day long it was 'Come, Fantasti-Calf! Let's go, Fantasti-Calf! Nice work, Fantasti-Calf!'"

"*Psst! Fantasti-Calf!*" came a familiar voice from the other side of the playground wall. The top of Norman's head rose into view, peeking at them through his yellow IncrediBull mask.

"Uggghhh...why are you here?" Dakota groaned. "Don't you get *tired*?"

"Evil never sleeps, Fantasti-Calf," Norman

said, "so neither do I! Besides, I've found the villain who's stolen our powers!"

"Who?" Chuck popped up, curious how Norman discovered who had stolen superpowers that didn't exist.

"Shhh!" Norman shushed, looking around secretively. He then pointed into the village at Wilhelm Wellington, proudly strutting toward the town square. "*Him*," he whispered. "*Count Chaos!*"

As usual, Dakota looked confused. Chuck flipped through his cowmic book and stopped on a page showing Count Chaos: a wide, gray bull dressed in a frilly black suit with a high-collared cape. He had heavy horns, a proud chest, and angry yellow eyes. He certainly *looked* like Wilhelm, except for the costume.

Dakota lowered the book and shook his head. "No, that's Wilhelm Wellington," he told Norman. "The richest bull on the island."

"A clever disguise, no doubt," Norman said, "but not clever enough to fool me. He's *Count Chaos*, a super villain, and he's stolen our—"

"Hey!" Patty suddenly yelled from the

other side of the playground. *"It's IncrediBull!"*

Every head in sight turned in their direction. Before you could say "Geronimoooo," Chuck and Dakota were nearly trampled by a small stampede of eager calves rushing to meet the real-life superhero. They surrounded Norman, chattering and mooing as many questions as they could think of.

Dakota couldn't believe how easily everyone was fooled by a fat bull in a swimsuit and cape. "Doesn't anyone notice how much...fluffier he is than IncrediBull?" he asked Chuck.

"Every calf needs something amazing to believe in," Chuck said. "Besides, he *has* been saving folks. Sort of."

"But that costume is terrible!" Dakota argued. "How can anyone not see that?"

Chuck raised his brows at Dakota, who glanced down at his own daily costume—the tattered cowmouflage with its big, ugly stitches and clunky coconut hooves.

"Oh," he murmured. "Never mind."

"*Hoi cow'a*, my young friends! *So long*...until next issue!" they overheard Norman telling the calves. "Study hard, keep yourselves

80

strong, and who knows? One of *you* might be a superhero!" He looked right at Dakota and gave a very obvious wink. Dakota buried his embarrassed face in his hands.

"Oh brother," he moaned.

✸ ✸ ✸

The next few days kept Chuck and Dakota very busy. Every day after class, Dakota put on his blue Fantasti-Calf mask, caped himself in a blue blanket, and went about the tiring task of keeping a fake superhero from getting into real trouble. Chuck followed along with his last issue of *IncrediBull*, coaching Dakota on how to play the part of a super sidekick. They both worried that they were spending too much time babysitting Norman and not enough time finding ways to get his memory back.

Norman soon grew tired of simple good deeds. Before long, he was in search of more daring acts of heroism...and he found them.

First was the florist fire. One evening, Miss Petunia kicked over a burning lantern in her flower shop when spooked by a big, hairy spider. The building erupted in flames, threatening to catch the whole village on fire. With a loud *"Geronimoooo,"* Norman dashed into the burning shop to save Miss Petunia, while his "sidekicks" fought the fire with the UdderTube—a gadget that worked a lot like a fire hose. Miss Petunia was quite thankful, despite the fact that Norman accidentally soaked the poor heifer with gallons and gallons of water.

"Moohalo, IncrediBull," Miss Petunia sobbed with water running into her eyes.

"If only the sunglobes weren't so dim, I wouldn't have had to light that lantern in the first place."

"Glad I could help, ma'am," Norman said, stomping embers from his cape. "Take care now...until next issue."

Then came the runaway raft. Chuck and Dakota's fuzzy classmate Muster was paddling his homemade raft for a sunset cruise when a strong current swept him toward the dangerous rocks offshore. Norman spotted him from the cliff above and leaped to the rescue. He quickly removed his mootility belt and dove into the water near the raft with a long *"Geronimooooooooo,"* followed by an enormous splash.

Right away, he started thrashing around in the waves and looking for something to grab on to. As he grasped the corner of Muster's raft, it became obvious that while IncrediBull was very brave, Norman did not know how to swim.

Chuck and Dakota clambered down to the rocky shore, all the while wondering why a bull who couldn't swim would own a striped yellow swimsuit. Dakota cast the Grapplehoof out into the water like a fishing pole, catching Norman by the tail. He reeled Norman in like a big red fish on a hook, while Norman pulled Muster's raft behind him.

"*Moohalo*, IncrediBull!" Muster sputtered when they reached the safety of the shore. "I can't believe I thought you weren't real! I was trying to paddle toward the shore, but the sunglobe in the lighthouse kept dimming.

And then I lost sight of which way I was going, and then that monster current got me, and then—"

"Just be safe from now on, son," Norman interrupted as seawater leaked from his nostrils. "*Hoi cow'a*—so long...until next issue."

Finally, there was the Cattle Car. It was a short, red trolley that carried a half-dozen or so cows and had a cycle attached to the front. The cycle was pedaled by a hefty black ox named Toro, who carted folks around the island in the trolley like a taxi. Toro was strong, sturdy, and fully capable of pulling the weight of six cows. But on this day, he was distracted by the weakening power of the chatterbox on his handlebars. He fiddled with the knob as he pedaled up the mountain, trying to turn up the volume on the radio. Suddenly, his front wheel bumped a big rock in the road, jostling the whole trolley. The cart broke loose from the cycle and careened backward down the side of Mount Maverick with a full load of passengers shrieking in panic.

Norman appeared out of nowhere wearing Hopperhooves—springy boots he had built that made him run twice as fast and jump twice as high as a normal cow. He hurdled after the runaway trolley, pounced through the air, and landed on the Cattle Car's roof with a single bound.

"*Geronimooooooooo!*" Norman cried as the cart sped down the mountain.

The trolley was zooming downhill too fast for Chuck and Dakota to help this time. Norman crawled onto the back end of the car as it veered off the road toward a thick cedar tree. He planted his big, wide legs into the ground, and a massive cloud of dirt and pebbles flew into the air from his hooves as he tried to stop the speeding trolley. The springs in Norman's Hopperhooves bounced back against the cart enough to slow it down, but not enough to stop it. The

Cattle Car hit a rock, bounced into the air, and crashed into the tree with Norman as a cushion.

When Chuck and Dakota finally caught up, they found Norman pinned between the trolley and the tree. The passengers were shaken up and Norman had a chipped horn, but otherwise everyone seemed to be okay. Toro finally arrived on his cycle and helped pull the trolley off Norman.

"That was amazing, IncrediBull," Toro said. "You saved everyone and didn't even damage my trolley...too much."

"Happy...to be...of service." Norman huffed and whimpered as he stood up and cracked his back. "So long, folks. Until...next...issue."

"We *have* to bring his memory back soon," Chuck said. "This is getting dangerous!"

"What does 'until next issue' mean?" Dakota asked. "Norman keeps saying that to everyone."

"It's at the end of every *IncrediBull*," Chuck said. He handed Dakota the rumpled cowmic book from his shirt pocket and flipped to the last ragged page. The final frame showed IncrediBull fighting a giant opossum with eight monstrous tails, while Count Chaos stood by and laughed evilly. Underneath the picture, a word bubble read:

Will IncrediBull defeat the dreaded Octopossum? Will Count Chaos rule the island? Find out next time! So long, reader... until next issue!

Dakota heard Norman groan as he held his aching back with one hoof and ran the other hoof over his chipped horn. "At the rate Norman's going, he might not *have* another issue."

"There's *always* another issue," Chuck insisted, taking back the cowmic book. He closed it and eyed the cover, and a sudden idea sprang into his head.

"That's it!" Chuck mooed. "Another issue! *Lots* of issues! *That's* how we'll get his memory back!" His tail swirled and twitched. "We need to get Norman back to his studio. I have an idea!"

7

SHARING GIFTS

Chuck and Dakota fetched the map from their winning ticket and brought Norman back to his house. Chuck's idea was for Dakota to show Norman every scrap of IncrediBull artwork in the studio, so he could see their adventures didn't exist anywhere but on paper. It seemed like a good idea. But no matter how many cowmic books, drawings, and posters they paraded in front of him, Norman still wasn't getting it.

"Look! See?" Dakota urged Norman, flipping pages in front of him. "IncrediBull *isn't real*. There are *no adventures*. These cowmic books prove it!"

"How can I not be real? I'm standing right here!" Norman pounded his chest. "Besides, this *whole house* is filled with trophies from our *very real* adventures." He took the book

from Dakota's hands and squinted at it. "Whoever drew this got a great likeness of me though. Except for the nose...far too big."

Dakota grunted with frustration and plopped onto the dusty couch. "You can't keep doing this! Don't you realize you're going to get hurt?"

"I have no choice," Norman said in a heroic voice. "I have a gift. Or I *used* to, anyway. Sharing it for the greater good is my only way to have a role in this society."

Dakota remembered the lesson Miss Ginger had taught them about talents. Norman was using IncrediBull's special abilities to help everyone around him. He recalled how thankful Soward was when they untangled him from his hammock, even though he ended up covered in cactus. Even when things didn't go according to plan, everyone still appreciated IncrediBull's effort.

"If that's the case, why don't you take off the mask and show who you really are?" Dakota asked.

"Excellent question, my young friend," Norman said, folding his big arms. "Why don't *you*?"

Dakota knew that Norman was talking about the blue Fantasti-Calf mask he'd been wearing for the last few days. But as a hu'man, Dakota couldn't help but think about the cow mask that he hid behind *every* day...and he knew exactly why it stayed on.

"Because folks would still be afraid," Dakota admitted quietly. "Even though we only want to help, the ones we love would still be afraid of how different we are."

"Exactly," Norman said. He joined Dakota on the couch, which sank under his weight. "You have a good heart, Fantasti-Calf. You know as well as I do what it's like to be a stranger in a strange land."

And there it was. Dakota was finally starting to understand. IncrediBull wasn't just some goofy hero looking for adventure. IncrediBull was an outsider, just like him. He was the only one of his kind, hiding behind a costume while trying to fit in and find a place in his new home.

"Okay, check out this one!" Chuck suddenly appeared from the other room holding a device made of sticks, a rake head, and a crank with a handle.

Since Norman wasn't convinced by the cowmic books, Chuck started using Norman's inventions as a way to make him remember who he was. "This one scratches your back for you."

"Very impressive," Norman said while Chuck used the device. "Who made this?"

"*You* did," Chuck said. "Don't you remember? You made *all* these inventions!"

"No, little one—I made all *these* inventions," Norman pointed to his mootility belt. "But I must admit, I learned quite a bit from the contraptions in this place. Whoever constructed them must have been a genius."

Chuck and Dakota both hung their heads. Bringing Norman back to reality was much tougher than they had expected. For the next few hours, they practically turned the house upside down trying to find something else that might trigger his memory. But they couldn't find anything. No photo albums, no old letters...nothing but IncrediBull drawings, IncrediBull cowmics, and IncrediBull relics. It was like Norman had said on the tour: IncrediBull had been his whole life. Now—sitting on the couch with a cape, a mask, and a logo on his chest—it actually *was* his life.

"We're wasting time!" Norman insisted. "I already know who I am. When I get my powers back, I'll prove it to you. We should be investigating that power thief Count Chaos!"

"*Wilhelm Wellington*," Dakota corrected him.

"Whoever you say he is, he's shown some very suspicious behavior lately!" Norman replied.

97

Chuck's tail drooped. "Wait...Have you been *following* him?"

"All week long," Norman bragged. "He spends a *lot* of time poking around those tall, spinning giants on the southern part of the island."

"The windspinners?" Dakota said. "Of course he spends a lot of time there. He owns them!"

"He also has secret meetings with other villains during the day," Norman continued. "Well-dressed scoundrels who gather behind closed doors right in the middle of town!"

"That's the Herd," Chuck explained. "They meet together and make the laws on Bermooda. You know...laws? The rules we all live by?"

"Egad!" Norman jumped up from the

couch, his nostrils flaring. "He's even made his way into the government? This is worse than I thought! That fiend doesn't want to help society. He wants to *own* it!"

"Just stay away from Wilhelm Wellington," Dakota said. "Tailing him will only bring trouble."

"Ha!" Norman laughed, putting both hooves on his hips and thrusting out his chest. "I *live* for trouble!"

"Yes," Dakota sighed, looking at Norman's chipped horn. "We know."

8

CAGED

The next day was so uneventful that Chuck and Dakota couldn't help but worry. It was the last day before the weekend, and they should have been glad that nothing out of the ordinary had happened so far. Thankfully, Norman hadn't shown up at school again. But that almost made them worry even more, especially since they hadn't been able to find him all afternoon.

After searching nearly the whole island, they'd seen neither hide nor hair of Norman. The sun was now beginning to set, and the only place IncrediBull could be found was in the news reports warbling out of Bermooda's chatterboxes, whose radio waves sounded softer and softer as the boltage got weaker and weaker.

"I hope Norman didn't follow Wilhelm down to the windspinners again," Dakota fretted as they sat down on the swings of the empty schoolhouse playground.

"You heard the chatterboxes," Chuck said as he started swinging. "It's been a big week for IncrediBull. Fires, ocean currents, out-of-control trolleys...maybe he's finally getting some rest."

Dakota hoped Chuck was right. But his

hopes were dashed when Patty suddenly showed up, her voice trembling with both excitement and panic.

"Hey, guys! You gotta come see this!"

They jumped off the swings, ran to the playground wall, and looked down the road. Coming their way was Marigold Colvin, Bermooda's chief of police, pedaling her rickshaw. Chief Colvin's rickshaw looked a lot like the Cattle Car, but instead of holding a dozen passengers, it pulled a tiny

cage built for one...and today that cage was holding Norman.

"Oh..." Chuck mooed. "That can't be good."

A group of curious cattle followed Chief Colvin as she pedaled into town. No one could remember the last time someone was locked up in that cage, but they knew that the

only place it took anyone was to the Corral. The Corral was a pen that was half buried in the ground and surrounded by thick mud walls, and had a door made of heavy wooden bars. In short, the Corral was a jail.

Norman hadn't gotten some rest. He'd gotten arrested.

"What happened?" Dakota asked as the crowd of cattle passed by.

"IncrediBull broke into Wellington Manor!" Patty said. "Wilhelm caught him sneaking around inside his mansion!"

It was no wonder Norman had been arrested. Wilhelm Wellington was a very territorial bull. If there was one thing you didn't do, it was trespass on his private property...*especially* Wellington Manor. Chuck and Dakota joined the crowd of cattle following the rickshaw. When they reached the Corral, Wilhelm was already there, huffing and puffing to the Herd. Chuck and Dakota inched closer to hear better.

"Cattle like this need to be put out to pasture," Wilhelm scolded. "There is simply no place on Bermooda for mad cows who run amok and cause trouble."

"Trouble?" Dakota piped up from the back of the crowd. "Ever since he showed up, the only thing he's done is help everyone!"

"Is that the *only* thing?" Wilhelm replied with a wicked smirk. "Have you not noticed the sorry state of our boltage?" He pointed to all the wavering sunglobes in the town square. "This 'hero' has been sneaking around my windspinners all week! Since he appeared, our lights have suddenly grown dimmer. Do you really think that's just a cow-incidence?"

"Don't listen to him!" Norman mooed. "He's not who you think he is! He's *Count Chaos*, a power-stealing super villain!"

The confused cattle all looked at each other. No one knew what to think. Then, as if on cue, all the sunglobes suddenly stopped flickering and went out completely. Every chatterbox in earshot wound down and went silent. The power was no longer weak. The power was gone.

"You see?" Wilhelm said. "This fellow is clearly out of his mind. Who knows what he has done to our boltage? Who knows what he might have done if I hadn't caught him in my home? Who knows what he may still do if we continue to let him run free!"

If there was one thing Wilhelm was talented at, it was giving speeches. The Herd members began snorting and stomping in agreement.

Chief Colvin calmed everyone down as best she could. "Having no boltage is not the end of the world," she assured the crowd while unlocking Norman's cage. "Let's not have a stampede here. Go home, light a torch, and we will deal with this in the morning."

With that, she led Norman down into the Corral and put him in his cell, where the only light was from the last rays of sunset coming through a tiny window.

Did I really make all this happen? Norman wondered to himself. He didn't think he had. But the past week was such a blur in his mind.

"What's going to happen now?" he asked

Chief Colvin through the wooden bars of the cell door.

"I don't know," she snorted, lighting a lantern on the wall. "I can't remember the last time we jailed someone. This is Bermooda. There are never any criminals here."

Norman's head hung low as his hooves gripped the bars. "Until now," he whispered sadly.

Outside the Corral, Dakota and Chuck tried to figure out what to do next.

"Nothing but trouble," Dakota ranted. "That's what I told him this would bring. So what does he do? Breaks into Wellington Manor! What does he find? Nothing... but...*trouble*!"

"What if Norman's right?" Chuck asked. "What if Wilhelm is up to something?"

"Like what?" Dakota said. "Wilhelm may be a first-class creep, but a *super villain*?"

"Well, he's definitely a liar," Chuck said. "The lights were dimming before Norman even hit his head, remember?"

Dakota recalled the flickering sunglobe on the studio tour—the one he had tried to fix. "That's true," he said thoughtfully. "That's how this whole thing started. IncrediBull didn't cause the power problem. The power problem caused IncrediBull! Why would Wilhelm lie about that?"

"Well, there's one way to find out. We're going to follow in Norman's hoofprints," Chuck said. "We're going to break into Wellington Manor."

WELLINGTON MANOR

All of Bermooda knew where Wellington Manor was. It was a huge, sprawling mansion on the south side of the mountain, not far from the grass farms and windspinners at Wellington Field. Tonight, however, it was even easier to spot than usual. As the rest of Bermooda softly lit up the evening with torches and candles, Wellington Manor glowed brightly with sunglobes that were not dim or flickering in the least.

"I *told* you something was wrong here," Chuck said as they crouched in the bushes outside. "Why is this place all lit up when everything else is dark?"

He tightened the cape now tied around his neck. Chuck had insisted they stop off at the Porter House so he could put together his own superhero outfit before they broke

into Wilhelm's mansion. He claimed it was to protect his identity. Truthfully, he was just tired of being the only one without a costume. He now crept toward the mansion wearing a bright green cape, swim goggles, and a crash helmet that had "Cowlossus" written on it.

"Who's 'Cowlossus'?" Dakota asked. "'You never mentioned a character named Cowlossus."

"I just made him up," Chuck whispered as they snuck under the windows. "He's Fantasti-Calf's long-lost brother. He can grow taller than a palm tree and wider than—"

"But you're only four feet tall," Dakota interrupted.

"That's because *someone stole my powers*, just like yours," Chuck said, crossing his arms.

The two small heroes wondered how to get in. All the windows were closed and locked. There were lots of balconies, but they were at least two stories up...and as Dakota had noted, he and Chuck were only four feet tall. Even if one of them stood on the other's shoulders, they wouldn't be tall enough. Chuck's tail twitched as usual, but he didn't have any ideas this time. Suddenly, Dakota spotted a familiar canvas belt stuck in the bushes under one of the balconies—the only balcony with an open door.

"Norman's mootility belt!" Dakota whispered. He looked up at the lit doorway of the balcony overhead. "Looks like he dropped everything. This must be how he got in."

"Get on my shoulders!" Chuck said, detaching the Hopperhooves from the back of the belt. "If these things can make a big bull like Norman jump high, imagine how high we can go!"

Dakota picked up the mootility belt and climbed onto Chuck's shoulders. Chuck took a good strong jump and found that one bounce was enough to send them rocketing up to the balcony. Dakota grabbed the railing tightly, with Chuck dangling from his feet. Climbing up Dakota like a rope ladder, Chuck made it to the railing, and they both pulled themselves over. They landed in a heap on the balcony.

"Well, that sure worked!" Chuck grunted, climbing to his feet. When they stood up, they found Norman's Grapplehoof lying on the balcony, followed by a trail of large cow tracks leading into the open door.

"This is how Norman got in," Dakota whispered, picking up the Grapplehoof. "We really are following in his hoofprints."

"There's one difference," Chuck said quietly as they entered the doorway. "We're not going to get caught."

The location of Wellington Manor may not have been secretive, but the inside of it sure was. Wilhelm didn't let many folks cross his doorway without good reason. Since neither Chuck nor Dakota ever had good reason, this was the first time either of them was seeing it. Put simply, it was incredible.

Most buildings on Bermooda were made of bamboo and clay, but Wellington Manor was made of richer woods like cherry, cedar, and mahogany. The ceilings were high, the hallways were wide, and the floors were made from precious stone that had been mined from within Mount Maverick. Everything had its place, and everything was *very* clean. But the strangest thing about this big house was that Chuck and Dakota seemed to be the only ones in it.

Wellington Manor was full of fancy objects. The first hallway they went through was lined with statues that sang as they walked past. By the time they reached the last statue, the whole hall sounded like a symphony. The next floor down had a dressing room with a tall, ornate mirror on the wall. Whenever they looked into it, a cheery voice rang out, "You're incredible, sir." When they reached the ground floor, they found a giant fountain bubbling in the middle of the parlor, brightly lit with colored sunglobes.

"What a waste!" Dakota said. "Singing statues, talking mirrors...and how many lights are in this fountain? Does all this stuff run on boltage? No wonder the whole island has gone out!"

"It is a big waste," Chuck said, "but I don't know if it's enough to soak up all the power on the island. It seems weird that there aren't any servants or maids here, doesn't it? This is a really big place, so who cleans it up?" Chuck had hardly finished his thought when they were surprised by the sudden appearance of another gadget—a mechanical cow that sputtered right up to them as if it were awaiting orders.

Instead of legs, it balanced on a single wheel. It had wooden arms that turned on gears and pulleys, with metal claws attached to the end. Its head looked like a bowl, and its body looked like an upside-down washtub. Rubber wires looped out from the sides of its head. Glowing eyes bugged out from the front, and two sunglobes burned brightly where the horns should have been. It didn't look like anything they had seen here so far, but it did look just like something they had recently seen in a drawing.

"Norman's autocow!" Chuck gasped. "It really *did* get stolen!"

"*Stolen*," came a robotic voice from inside the autocow's head. "*The condition of property that has been taken without permission.*"

"It can talk!" Dakota marveled. "Can it think too? Does it know where it came from?"

"*Where it came from,*" the autocow repeated. It rolled down the hallway toward the front foyer. "*Where it came from... Where it came from...*"

It unlocked the door and rolled outside, crossing the wide front pasture with Chuck and Dakota following behind. Leaves smacked them in the face as it led them through the trees to a small hillside cave. It paused for a moment, looked back at them, then disappeared into the dark entrance, its voice still beckoning them to follow.

"*Where it came from... Where it came from...*"

10

JAILBREAK

The noisy autocow bleeped and blooped as it led Chuck and Dakota down a long, dark tunnel with its glowing eyes lighting the way. It bounced along, repeating the same two words over and over again:

"Came from...came from...came from..."

"It sounds like a broken record," Dakota said. "Is something wrong with it?"

"It seems to know where it's going,"

Chuck answered.

The autocow finally rolled to a stop at a rock wall at the end of the tunnel.

"Great," Dakota huffed. "We came all the way down here for nothing! I *knew* this thing was broken."

"*Broken*," the autocow recited. *"Fractured. Faulty. Not functioning properly."*

"We could have gone home instead of breaking into Wellington Manor," Dakota continued griping. "But noooo...we just had to push it."

"*Push it*," the autocow repeated. "*Push it... push it...*"

The babbling robot pushed against the wall and one of the boulders slid forward, revealing a secret room.

"*Where it came from*," the autocow repeated one last time.

"I'm sure this thing is strong"—Dakota ran his hand along the autocow's arm—"but strong enough to push a *boulder*?"

Chuck put his ear up to the boulder and knocked on the side. An empty echo rang back at him. "It's hollow!" he said. "This boulder probably weighs less than we do!"

Chuck and Dakota couldn't see much in the darkness. They were in some kind of huge, domed chamber that had been dug underground. In front of them was a tall scaffolding lashed together from palm trees. It stood in the middle of the cavern, its winding stairs gently lit by moonlight that filtered in through a big grate in the dirt ceiling high above.

"What's that noise?" Chuck asked. A steady hum was coming from the top of the scaffold. They crept carefully up the stairs in the dark. When they reached the top platform, they found the source of the noise was a contraption unlike any they'd ever seen.

It was a big rack that stood at least eight feet tall and ten feet wide. It was filled with hundreds of small tubes that looked like spools of thread connected by rubber wires. The machine was dotted here and there with buttons, gauges, and glowing sunglobes. In the middle was a big, red dial with the words "Main Power," from which a big cable ran up to the ceiling and out of the grate. Chuck and Dakota studied the grate, both thinking same thing: *Where does that cable go?*

Dakota slung the mootility belt over his shoulder and shimmied up the cable to the grate, which was made from thick bamboo shoots. With his feet dangling, he grabbed its bars in his hands, stuck his head through the grate, and looked around. He saw the outline of Mount Maverick above them, and the place where the light on top of the radio tower should have been. But it was dark, just like everything else. He followed the cable with his eyes all the way to a squat, square building surrounded by tall windspinners, whose woven blades spun quickly in the night breeze.

"We're under Wellington Field!" Dakota called out. "The cable goes to a little building in the middle of all the windspinners!"

"That's the power station." Chuck scratched his chin. "It collects all the boltage from the windspinners and sends it out to the island. No wonder everything's gone dark! Wilhelm really *is* stealing power!"

"So what's *that* thing?" Dakota asked, poking his head back inside and looking at the machine with its collection of tubes and wires. "Why does it need so much boltage?"

"It's called a cow-puter," a deep voice answered from the dark edge of the platform. Chuck and Dakota froze, with Dakota still hanging from the grate overhead. Out of the shadows stepped Wilhelm Wellington, looking even more smug than usual. "The reason it needs so much boltage is because it feeds my many, *many* children." He pulled a lever on the machine and the whole chamber lit up, revealing something that Chuck and Dakota had completely missed in the thick darkness.

Looking down, they no longer saw *one* autocow. They saw *dozens* of autocows.

Hundreds of them, in fact...maybe even more. It was like a Bermooda-sized herd of mechanical cows, each one with its head turned up and eyes glowing. They all stood neatly in rows, attached to the cow-puter with long wires that ran up the middle of the scaffold. Chuck and Dakota felt the color drain from their faces.

Wilhelm clutched Chuck's shirt and lifted him up, looking closely at his helmet. "I don't know who you are, Cowlossus, but you are *trespassing.*" He tossed Chuck from the scaffold platform all the way down to the ground, where he was caught by the army of autocows. Their arms may have only been made of wood, but their gears and springs were all wound tightly. Chuck was quickly locked in a grip that was impossible to escape.

the building. She set her pineapple down by the door and walked around to investigate. All she saw was her rickshaw parked along the side of the building. What she didn't see was Dakota hiding behind the corner, doing his best to whistle while out of breath from his run across the island. She didn't see him gripping the Grapplehoof in his hands. And she didn't see the Hopperhooves that he had propped under the rickshaw's back wheels.

Dakota needed Norman's help. But first he needed to break Norman out of jail. The adventures of the past week had given Dakota an idea of how to distract the Chief for a while. The springs in Norman's boots had been powerful enough to slow down a speeding cart. Maybe they'd be strong enough to make a stopped cart speed up.

As the Chief edged closer, Dakota took careful aim, launched the Grcapplehoof at the Hopperhooves, and...

Sproiiinnnggg! The boots released their springs, firing the rickshaw backward with tremendous force. It shot through Bermooda Village like a rocket, with Chief Colvin racing after it.

"Stop! Stop!" she cried as the driverless rickshaw tore through the fruit stand where she had bought her pineapple and rolled out of sight at full speed.

Dakota knew he might not have much time. He crept around front, where the keys were still in the lock of the Corral door. He opened the door, and there he found Norman wallowing in his cell with his big head in his hooves. Dakota pulled

the keys from the front door and unlocked
Norman's cell, and the gate swung wide
open. Dakota scratched his head in
amazement. He'd always imagined a jail-
break would be much harder than this.
But Norman didn't budge.

"Come on, IncrediBull," Dakota said.
"Bermooda needs a hero."

"Go away," Norman said, sulking. "I'm
no hero. I killed the island's boltage."

"No you didn't!" Dakota quickly rambled. "My brother Chuck—er—*Cowlossus* and I found out that Wilhelm—er—*Captain Chaos* has been draining it all for himself!"

"Your brother?" Norman said, squinting.

"You were right!" Dakota said. "Captain Chaos really is stealing power! Just not the kind you suspected."

Norman wrinkled his nose. "Fantasti-Calf has a brother?"

Dakota waved his hands. "Yeah, he can grow taller than a palm tree and...Oh, never mind! Just come on! I brought your IncrediBelt."

"I don't want that thing," Norman grumbled. "It's just another reminder that I have no powers. No gifts. Nothing to offer anyone."

"We all have gifts," Dakota said, "and

they're not always about what we can do. Something our gifts are about what we are."

"A disgrace is what I am," Norman muttered. "I tried to help everyone, and now they're all mad at me. You were right. There's no adventure. Bermooda has no need for IncrediBull."

"Yesterday, you jumped on a speeding cart to save a dozen cows that you didn't even know," Dakota reminded him. "And you did it without any powers. Your gift to Bermooda isn't flight or speed...or even the gadgets in this belt. It's *courage*. Courage and caring. That's exactly what Bermooda needs right now."

"Why?" Norman raised his brow.

"Because right now, Count Chaos is draining boltage to power his own army of robots," Dakota said. "And they're holding my brother prisoner in a secret underground hideout!"

Norman straightened up. This adventure did sound tempting, but he still wasn't sure about breaking out of jail.

Dakota sighed. "And because if you help me, we might be able to get our powers back."

"What are we waiting for?" Norman thundered, leaping to his feet. "*Geronim—*"

"Shhh!" Dakota shushed him.

Norman whispered, "Geronimooooo."

They peeked out the front door. There was no sign of Chief Colvin. The rickshaw must have rolled all the way to the edge of town.

"I'm a fugitive," Norman said sadly, looking back at his cell. "What do I do now?"

Dakota spotted Soward Seawell rolling a

barrel of corn oil across the road—fuel for his prized airplane, no doubt.

"Now you grab that pineapple," Dakota said. "We're going to see a friend about a favor with no questions asked."

11

MORE THAN AN ARMY

"All in all, this couldn't have worked out better," Wilhelm gloated as he came down the scaffold steps. "I've noticed your big, red friend following me all week. I was planning to set up some kind of trap for him. Instead, the big lummox breaks into my mansion and gets himself caught. Now everyone thinks he's to blame for the power loss!"

He laughed with a cackle evil enough to

be worthy of Count Chaos. The horde of autocows even joined in with a robotic: "*Ha-ha-ha-ha-ha...*"

"You're stealing all the boltage just so you can have your own private army?" Chuck said.

"An army? Is that all you see?" Wilhelm sneered. He waved his arm over the legion of autocows standing in formation. "This is the *future*! Servants who can work endlessly, needing nothing in return but a little boltage. Just imagine! A whole race of mechanical cows that can perform all the same talents as real ones! Machines that build! Machines that farm! Machines that cook, clean, and serve snacks by the pool!"

Chuck craned his neck to get a better look at the robots. Indeed, they each appeared to be designed for different purposes. Some of them were farmers, with pitchforks and cutting blades attached to their arms. Some were mechanics, carrying a collection of wrenches and pointy screwdrivers. Some were construction workers, equipped with saws, drills, and even jackhammers.

"It's much more than an army, little friend." Wilhelm lowered his voice. "It's a society! My very own society...with me as its king. With these autocows, I no longer need the talents or skills of anyone. Not you, your shaggy red friend, or anyone else on this island."

Chuck wondered what everyone on Bermooda would do when they found out they had all been replaced. But even more, he wondered why Wilhelm was telling his whole plan. Maybe he just liked the sound of his own voice. But Chuck suspected it was because Wilhelm wasn't planning on letting him leave...ever.

* * *

Dakota knew they'd never get back to the tunnel in time by traveling on foot. Springing Norman from jail had taken long enough, and Wilhelm might even have the tunnel guarded by now. Instead, they were flying right to Wilhelm's lair in Soward's airplane, the *Hawk*.

Getting Soward's help was easier than Dakota had expected. IncrediBull may have been an escaped prisoner, but Soward couldn't resist the pineapple that Dakota brought him. Besides, he *had* promised IncrediBull a favor.

"I know I said no questions asked," Soward squealed, "but where do you need me to land this old bird?"

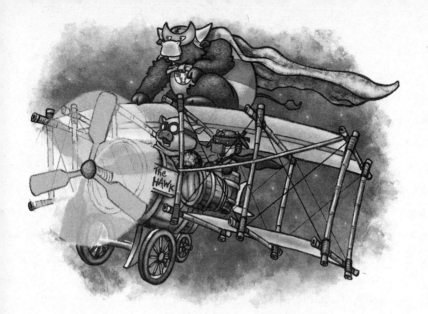

"Take us to the windspinners at Wellington Field!" Dakota shouted over the *Hawk*'s engine. "We won't need you to land. We just need you to drop us off!"

Dakota wasn't sure why Wilhelm had his own robot army. But he was secretly stealing the island's boltage to do it, and he had taken Chuck captive...so Dakota had a feeling that it wasn't for anything good. He just hoped that they weren't too late.

Meanwhile, Wilhelm was still giving his long-winded victory speech. He really loved giving speeches. He yammered on and on until Chuck thought his brain might melt if he had to hear any more. Chuck wondered if this never-ending blabber was Wilhelm's way of torturing him.

"This will bring about a new Bermooda," Wilhelm droned, "a perfect one...with everything following my own design—"

Wilhelm's speech was cut off by a growing noise outside. It sounded like some kind of engine coming from the sky. Squinting through the grate high up in the ceiling, Wilhelm made out the shape of Soward's plane swooping ever closer.

"I say," Wilhelm muttered. "Is that a bird?"

"*Negative*," the autocow holding Chuck chirped. "*It is a plane.*"

"You're both wrong." Chuck grinned at the moonlit figure standing atop the *Hawk* with its cape flapping in the wind. "It's *IncrediBull!*"

"*Geronimooooooooo!*" Norman's voice bellowed into the night air as he and Dakota leaped from Soward's airplane. They crashed through the bamboo grate and slid down one of the big wooden pilings, right into the middle of the autocows.

Wilhelm was outraged to see Norman out of the Corral. He hated seeing one of his schemes fail.

"*Stop them!*" he commanded the autocows, snorting and stomping and shaking his cane. "*Crush them! Finish them all!*"

The autocows were all attached to the cow-puter with wires, but they could still move around enough to be menacing. They surrounded Norman and Dakota with claws snapping, saws buzzing, and blades pointing. Wilhelm may have planned to make these robots a society, but right now they were an army.

Although Norman wasn't a real super-hero, he was a really big bull. And if there was one thing he was great at, it was making a huge mess. He plowed through the swarm of autocows, swinging his heavy arms wildly. Dakota was impressed at how quickly Norman reduced the autocows to spare parts. Gears and sprockets flew everywhere as he smashed robots to pieces by the dozen.

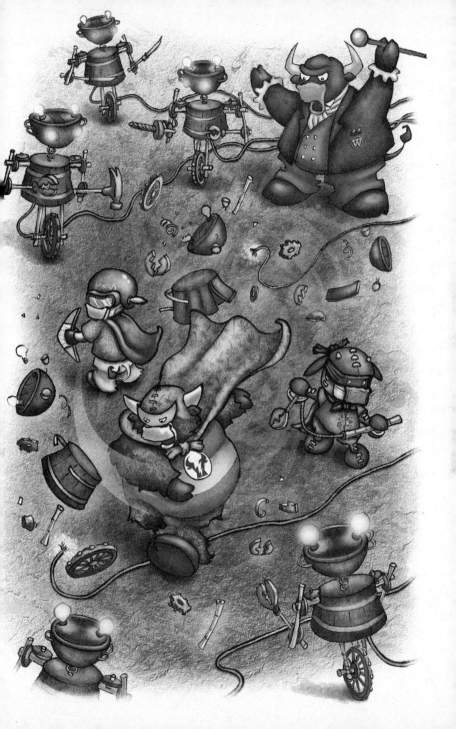

A stocky autocow that had obviously been designed for mining came at Dakota with a sharp pickax. Dakota swung the Grapplehoof in a circle over his head, lassoed the pickax, and gave a sharp pull.

"Sorry...all *mine*!" Norman joked as he yanked the pickax from the robot's claws. He then hurled it back at the autocow, punching a hole right through its middle.

Chuck felt his captor's arms loosen in all the confusion. He wiggled loose, ran to Norman, and grabbed the Mooberang from his belt. A construction autocow spotted Chuck and rolled toward him with two drills whirring at high speed. Chuck flung the Mooberang with surprisingly good aim for someone with hooves instead of hands. The spinning Mooberang sliced right through the autocow's glowing eyes, putting its lights out before returning to Chuck.

"Bull's-eye!" Chuck mooed, jumping onto the blind robot's shoulders. He gave a good strong kick, knocking the autocow's wooden head clean off its body.

Wilhelm's mouth was agape in disbelief. His perfect plan was falling apart, along with his autocows. He ran to the scaffold and rushed up the winding stairs.

"*Hey!*" Chuck hollered. "He's getting away!"

Norman charged through a half-dozen autocows, chasing after Wilhelm. But the steps were a bit rickety for big fellows like Wilhelm and Norman, and his huge hooves stamped a hole right through one of them.

"There's no escape for you, Count Chaos!" Norman roared, pulling his leg from the hole and carefully continuing the climb. "Today you will face bovine justice!"

Wilhelm rolled his eyes and groaned. Without a word, he clambered up the bamboo poles from the broken grate and escaped through the hole in the ceiling just as Norman reached the platform.

"That's odd," Norman said out loud, putting his hooves on his hips. "Villains almost always have something else to say. I'm rather disappointed."

"Forget about him!" Dakota yelled from below. "Do something about these autocows!" He and Chuck had gotten many of the robots to chase them in circles, knotting themselves up in their own wires. But there were still too many to fend off by themselves.

Norman looked at the big, red dial on the

computer. "Here's the Main Power dial," he said. "But which way should I turn it? Well, heroes always stand for what's right...right? I guess I should turn it to the right!" Norman spun the dial all the way to the right.

"That's the wrong way!" Dakota screamed. "That's *more* power!"

Chuck and Dakota watched in horror as a blue flow of boltage ran down the wires into every autocow in the cavern. But the sudden surge of power was too much for the robotic cows to handle. They all started shaking and vibrating and wheeling around in wobbly circles. Their eyes glowed brighter and brighter, until their bulbs popped in a spray of shattered glass. Then the autocows all fell over onto the ground and flopped around like fish suddenly plucked out of water.

A glowing spiderweb of tiny lightning bolts swarmed over them, until suddenly— *BOOM!* One of the autocows erupted in a small burst of smoke and flames. Chuck and Dakota took cover behind the fake boulder at the tunnel entrance just as a second one blew up, scattering robot parts everywhere. Then another and another and another...One by one, the autocows all started to explode, rocking the cavern walls and splintering the pilings that held up the ceiling. The whole room shook as clumps of dirt fell from above.

"This whole place is gonna cave in!" Dakota cried. "We have to unplug all those autocows!"

Chuck's tail twitched as he looked at the Mooberang still in his hooves. "No," he said, "we just have to unplug the power!" He threw the Mooberang with the same expert aim that had knocked out the autocow's eyes. It struck the power cable coming from outside, knocking it loose from the cow-puter in a shower of sparks.

Without power, the big machine went silent and whichever autocows hadn't blown up yet went completely limp on the ground. Looking through the smashed grate in the ceiling, Dakota could see the light on top of the radio tower glowing brightly once again. Power had been returned to the island.

It was too late to stop the collapsing cavern, however. The exploding autocows had caused too much damage. Bigger and bigger chunks dropped onto their heads as the ceiling began to come down.

"Quick! Through the tunnel!" Dakota

grabbed the hollow boulder with both hands and easily hoisted it over his head.

"Come on, IncrediBull!" Chuck shouted up to Norman. "The power is back! We have to take off!"

Norman gazed down in awe. Wearing his superhero costume and holding the giant boulder over his head, Dakota looked every bit like the super-strong Fantasti-Calf from the cover of *IncrediBull #35*.

"Ha-haaa!" Norman thundered. "Our power *is* back! It *is* time for takeoff! *Geronimooooooooooo!*" He ran to the edge of the shaky scaffolding, took a winning leap...and plummeted like a rock.

Norman had taken a lot of falls since he became IncrediBull, and the scaffolding was no higher than the cliffs that he had been heroically diving from all week. He probably would have been fine if he had landed on his round, jiggly belly or his big, squishy rump. But instead, he landed square on his head, knocking himself out cold.

"Did you really have to say 'takeoff'?" Dakota yelled as he ran to Norman and grabbed his left hoof.

"Don't complain, *Fantasti-Calf*," Chuck shot back, grabbing Norman's right hoof. "Just put some *calf muscle* into it!" They dragged Norman past the hollow boulder and safely into the tunnel just as the whole room rumbled and collapsed, filling the tunnel with a thick cloud of dirt and then...silence.

Chuck and Dakota wiped the dust from their faces. Wilhelm had escaped, but the cow-puter and the autocows were all buried under a heap of fallen earth. It was over. Norman was out like a light, and Chuck and Dakota had to lug him all the way down the dark tunnel. When they finally got to the entrance, they pulled Norman out of the cave and plopped down in the grass to take a breath of the cool night air.

"I can't believe it," Dakota panted, taking off his Fantasti-Calf mask. "That rotten Wilhelm got away."

"That's the way it is with super villains," Chuck said, tossing his helmet aside. "They *always* get away. At least until the next issue."

Just then, their shaggy red friend began to stir. "Ugghhhh..." Norman moaned as he cracked open his eyes and dragged himself to a sitting position. "Hey, what happened to my studio?" He looked down at his tattered costume. "And what am I wearing? This is the worst IncrediBull costume ever."

Chuck and Dakota heaved a sigh of relief. That hard landing on Norman's noggin had finally brought his memory back. IncrediBull was gone.

"Let's get you home," Chuck said. "We'll explain on the way."

12

UNTiL NEXT iSSUE

Chuck and Dakota no longer needed a map to find Norman's studio. After the events of the last few days, that dusty mess had begun to feel like their second home. Norman couldn't remember anything that had happened after the heavy statue fell on his head.

They decided it was best not to tell him the truth about his feats all over the island or that they had found his stolen autocow. After all, IncrediBull had escaped from jail; all the autocows were buried; and the only evidence of Wilhelm's plot was a big hole in the ground. Instead, they made up a story they knew Norman would love. It was the safest way to keep him out of trouble.

"So that's what happened," Chuck said, wrapping up their whopper as they approached Norman's studio. "You were showing us how easy it is to make our own IncrediBull costumes when a bunch of ships appeared in the sky. They took you up in a beam of light and then dropped you off out in that field."

"Looks like it really was aliens," Dakota added. "I guess they wanted to find out what you know about IncrediBull. The radiation from all those spaceships must have messed up the sunglobes and made you lose your memory."

"Duuuude...that's crazy," Norman mooed.

"Just like you said," Dakota answered, "there's all kinds of craziness out here."

"Well, thanks for finding me," Norman said. "*Moohalo.*"

The calves stopped short at the angry warning signs in the weedy yard. Now that Norman was himself again, they thought he might not want them coming back to break any more of his stuff.

"So long, Norman," Dakota said. "Get some sleep. You've had a big day."

"Nothing some coconut pudding can't fix," Norman smiled. Then he said something that surprised them. "Hey, you wanna join me?"

Chuck and Dakota looked at each other in shock.

"Really?" Chuck asked. "You don't want us to keep out?"

"Or go away'?" Dakota added.

Norman answered by pulling up the GO AWAY sign from the ground. "You dudes brought me home," he said. "I figure I can trust you."

"Actually, I think that kind of makes us friends," Dakota grunted as he yanked the KEEP OUT sign from the tall grass. "Doesn't it?"

Norman thought about that as Chuck joined them, removing the THIS MEANS YOU! sign from the yard. These two calves were his first visitors in quite some time (aside from the aliens, of course). For reasons he couldn't explain, he was oddly happy to have met them...and it had been a long while since he had some friends.

"Hey, I just had a great idea for a new superhero," Norman said, tucking the sign under his arm as they brushed through the weeds. "Cowlossus! Fantasti-Calf's long-lost brother, who can grow taller than a palm tree!"

Dakota's eyes widened. "Oh, that's...interesting. What made you think of that?"

"I dunno, dude," Norman shrugged. "These ideas just come to me."

"It's a good one," Chuck laughed, patting Norman on the arm.

With that, the three friends went inside for a hero's helping of coconut pudding. And as the door to Norman Redmane's well-lit studio closed, so did IncrediBull's amazing adventure on Bermooda...until next issue.

NOW iN PAPERBACK!

WELCOME TO BERMOODA #1: LOST iN BERMOODA

WELCOME TO BERMOODA

LOST iN BERMOODA

"LiTWIN PACKS A LOT OF ACTiON iNTO A LiTTLE BOOK."
—*Bulletin of the Center for Children's Books*, recommended

MiKE LiTWiN
New York Times bestselling illustrator

Lost in Bermooda • 978-0-8075-8717-1

Nobody knows Chuck Porter's new best friend Dakota is a hu'man (probably because he wears cowmouflage to make him look like a cow). But someone has been spreading rumors that there's a cow-eating hu'man on the island and the cowfolk are panicking! Does someone know about Dakota's true identity? Or is there another hu'man lurking around Bermooda? Chuck and Dakota are determined to find out!

PRAISE FOR *LOST IN BERMOODA*:

"Litwin's light tale of friendship is full of Hawaii-inspired cow puns and reads like the intro to a series... New-to-chapters readers will gladly join the herd and say 'Lo'hai' (hello) to Bermooda and its denizens."
—*Kirkus Reviews*

"In his debut as an author, illustrator Litwin (*My Name Is Not Isabella*) takes a goofy premise and runs with it... Litwin lays it on thick with the bovine puns...and the ample humor and some revelations about Dakota's backstory should leave readers looking forward to subsequent books."—*Publishers Weekly*

"Printed in short chapters of generously leaded type strewn with vignettes of a diverse anthropomorphic cast, Litwin's tale not only builds a properly suspenseful, storm-wrecked climax, but is udderly loaded with bovine wordplay. Only a 'kau'pai' would fail to chortle, and that's no bull."—*Booklist*

"Litwin packs a lot of action into a little book through the pair's attempts to get Dakota home, while still making both Chuck and Dakota well-rounded and adding bumps along the way in their relationship."
—*Bulletin of the Center for Children's Books*, recommended

Chuck and Dakota are setting sail on a high-sea adventure! The boys join local legend Marco Polo (a swashclucking rooster) on his quest for the Coral Crown, the most special treasure in the entire ocean. But the catfish bully the Kingfish wants the crown for himself and will do anything to get it. Can the buccowneers work together to find the treasure before the evil Kingfish finds them?

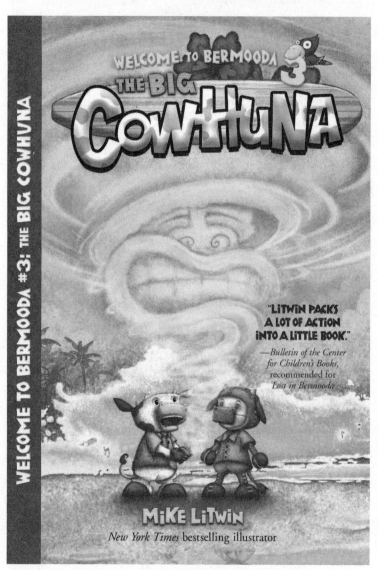

When Chuck and Dakota discover a mysterious seashell on the beach, they are swept into a whirlwind of adventure. Inside the shell is Zephyr, a talking tornado with the power to grant wishes! But when their wishes start to backfire, life in Bermooda goes bananas. Can Chuck and Dakota get everything back to normal before all the cows go mad?

MIKE LITWIN is a big kid disguised in a grown-up costume who gets paid to draw pictures all day. It pretty much rocks. He is the award-winning illustrator of *New York Times* bestsellers *My Name Is Not Isabella*, *My Name Is Not Alexander*, and *Isabella: Girl on the Go*. He lives in North Carolina with his wife and four children.